Dear Parents,

Welcome to the Scholastic Reader series. We have taken over 80 years of experience with teachers, parents, and children and put it into a program that is designed to match your child's interests and skills.

Level 1—Short sentences and stories made up of words kids can sound out using their phonics skills and words that are important to remember.

Level 2—Longer sentences and stories with words kids need to know and new "big" words that they will want to know.

Level 3—From sentences to paragraphs to longer stories, these books have large "chunks" of texts and are made up of a rich vocabulary.

Level 4—First chapter books with more words and fewer pictures.

It is important that children learn to read well enough to succeed in school and beyond. Here are ideas for reading this book with your child:

- Look at the book together. Encourage your child to read the title and make a prediction about the story.
- Read the book together. Encourage your child to sound out words when appropriate. When your child struggles, you can help by providing the word.
- Encourage your child to retell the story. This is a great way to check for comprehension.
- Have your child take the fluency test on the last page to check progress.

Scholastic Readers are designed to support your child's efforts to learn how to read at every age and every stage. Enjoy helping your child learn to read and love to read.

　　　　　—Francie Alexander
　　　　　　Chief Education Officer
　　　　　　Scholastic Education

™

THE BAD DOGS MEET FROM SPACE

BY **B.J. JAMES**

ILLUSTRATED BY **CHRIS DEMAREST**

For Devin
—B.J.J.

For Trish
—C.D.

No part of this publication may be reproduced, or stored in a retrieval system, or transmitted in any form or by any means, electronic, mechanical, photocopying, recording, or otherwise, without written permission of the publisher. For information regarding permission, write to Scholastic Inc., Attention: Permissions Department, 557 Broadway, New York, NY 10012.

Library of Congress Cataloging-in-Publication Data
James, B.J.
  Supertwins meet the bad dogs from space / by B.J. James; illustrated by Chris Demarest.
    p. cm. — (Scholastic reader! Level 2) "Cartwheel Books."
Summary: Young twin superheroes Timmy and Tabby battle laser-shooting space poodles who have come to take over Earth.
  ISBN 0-439-46623-7 (pbk. : alk. paper)
    [1. Heroes—Fiction. 2. Twins—Fiction. 3. Brothers and sisters—Fiction. 4. Extraterrestrial beings—Fiction. 5. Poodles—Fiction. 6. Dogs—Fiction.] I. Demarest, Chris L., ill. II. Title. III. Series
PZ7.J153585 Ss 2003
    398.2'0944'02—dc21
[Fic]—dc21
2002009313   CIP

12 11 10 9 8 7 6 5 4 3 2   03 04 05 06 07
          Printed in the U.S.A. 23 • First printing, May 2003

Scholastic Reader — Level 2

SCHOLASTIC INC.

New York Toronto London Auckland Sydney
Mexico City New Delhi Hong Kong Buenos Aires

Chapter 1

Tabby and I were walking
to school.
I looked up.
Three big poodles flew by!

I said, "This looks like trouble!"
"No, it doesn't," said Tabby.
"But you didn't even look!"
I said.

Sometimes, being a
Supertwin is hard—
even harder than
doing homework!

"Oh, no!" I yelled. "They could really hurt someone!"
"You are trying to trick me," said Tabby. "I won't look."

I shook my head. Sometimes fighting with sisters is harder than fighting bad guys.

She tried not to look. But I could tell she was peeking.

"Ahhhhh!" Tabby yelled.
"Poodles from space!
We have to do something,
Timmy," she said.

SMACK!

It was time to
send those dogs
back to space!

Tabby and I took out our capes.

And then we took off!
Up, up, and away!

SWOOSH

THEN...

POW!

The bad doggies went flying out of sight.

"We won!" we both shouted.
Then the bell rang.
Yikes!
We were late for school!

Chapter 2

At school,
I had an idea.
Those flying poodles will
come back.
That is what bad guys do.
They always come back.

"No talking, you two,"
Mrs. Shelly said.
Mrs. Shelly is our teacher.
She is the nicest teacher
in the whole first grade.
But she is not nice
when we are talking superhero
stuff during math.
Tabby and I stopped talking.

"We will go back,"
mean Mr. Bark said.
"That is what bad guys
do. We always go back!"

Tabby asked Mrs. Shelly
if we could leave.
"We have to save the world!"
I said.
"That can wait until recess,"
Mrs. Shelly said.

Soon it was time for recess.
The sky was filled with flying dog-ships.
Tabby knew what to do.

Tabby whispered her plan to me.
It was a good plan.

Tabby flew into the sky.
Rainbows shot out from her hands.
The doggies couldn't see.
I spun the ships around
and around.

They were going
fast, fast, fast.
It looked like fun!
But not for them!

Mean Mr. Bark was not happy.
He told all the dogs to fly away.
And they did.

We rushed back to the playground.
The other kids were already inside.
"Oh, no!" Tabby said.
Recess was over.
We had to hurry.

I told Tabby to tuck in her cape.
She always forgets.

Chapter 3

After school,
Tabby and I raced home.
She won.
She always wins.

At home,
our mom was in the
kitchen.
"Hello, kids.
How was school today?"
Mom asked.
Our mom is super cool!

"Timmy and I saved the world,"
Tabby said.
Tabby always tells Mom
when we save the world,
even though it is
supposed to be a secret.

"We flew really high.
And I shot rainbows
from my hands like this.
And . . ."

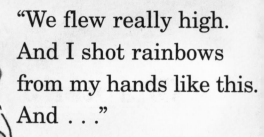

"That's nice," Mom said. "Do
you have homework?"
"Yes," we said.
"Okay. You can play again
when you are done,"
she said.
"Yes, Mom."

Even superheroes have to listen to their mothers!

Fluency Fun

The words in each list below end in the same sounds.
Read the words in a list.
Read them again.
Read them faster.
Try to read all 15 words in one minute.

fight	**book**	**found**
light	**cook**	**pound**
night	**look**	**sound**
right	**took**	**ground**
sight	**shook**	**around**

Look for these words in the story.

always   **world**   **sure**

idea   **couldn't**

Note to Parents:

According to *A Dictionary of Reading and Related Terms*, fluency is "the ability to read smoothly, easily, and readily with freedom from word-recognition problems." Fluency is necessary for good comprehension and enjoyable reading. The activities on this page include a speed drill and a sight-recognition drill. Speed drills build fluency because they help students rapidly recognize common syllables and spelling patterns in words, and they're fun! Sight-recognition drills help students smoothly and accurately recognize words. Practice these activities with your child to help him or her become a fluent reader.

—**Wiley Blevins,**
Reading Specialist